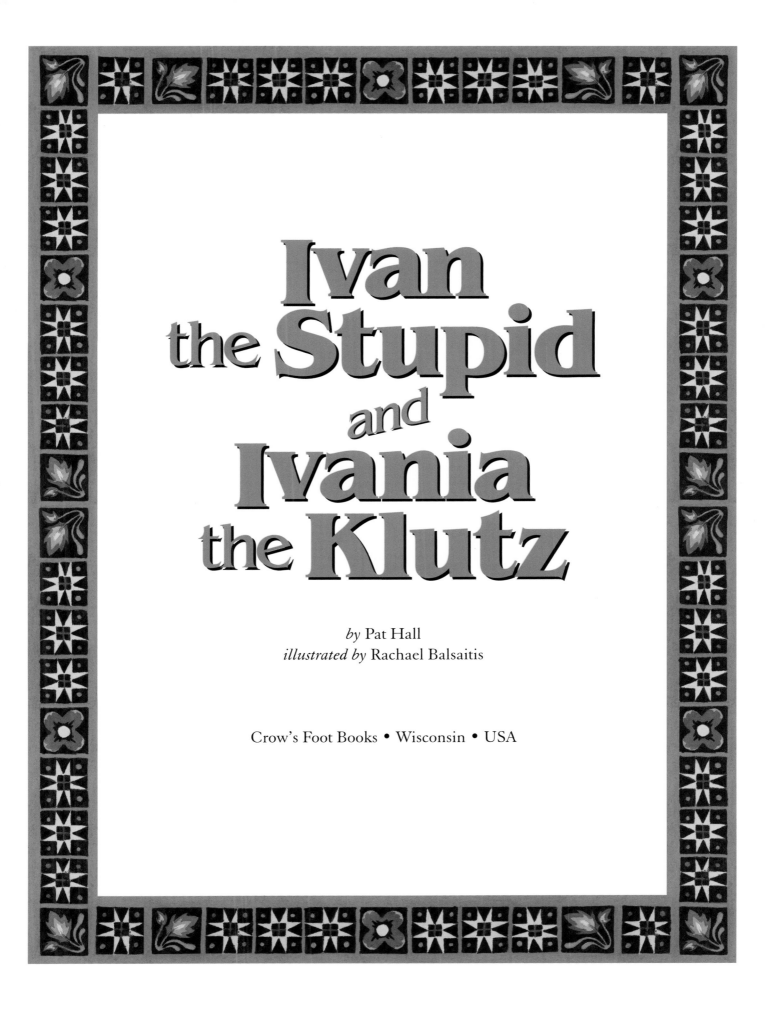

Ivan the Stupid and Ivania the Klutz

by Pat Hall
illustrated by Rachael Balsaitis

Crow's Foot Books • Wisconsin • USA

Crow's Foot Books
Janesville, Wisconsin
crowsfootbooks@gmail.com

Printed and bound in the United States of America
First Edition
10 9 8 7 6 5 4 3 2 1
LCCN 2019918797
ISBN 978-0-578-60863-1

This book was expertly produced by Book Bridge Press.
www.bookbridgepress.com

baba *[Russian] noun:*
an old woman,
a grandmother,
especially in fairy tales

To babas everywhere

And to Beth, whose gift was joy

—P. H.

For my dedushka

—R. B.

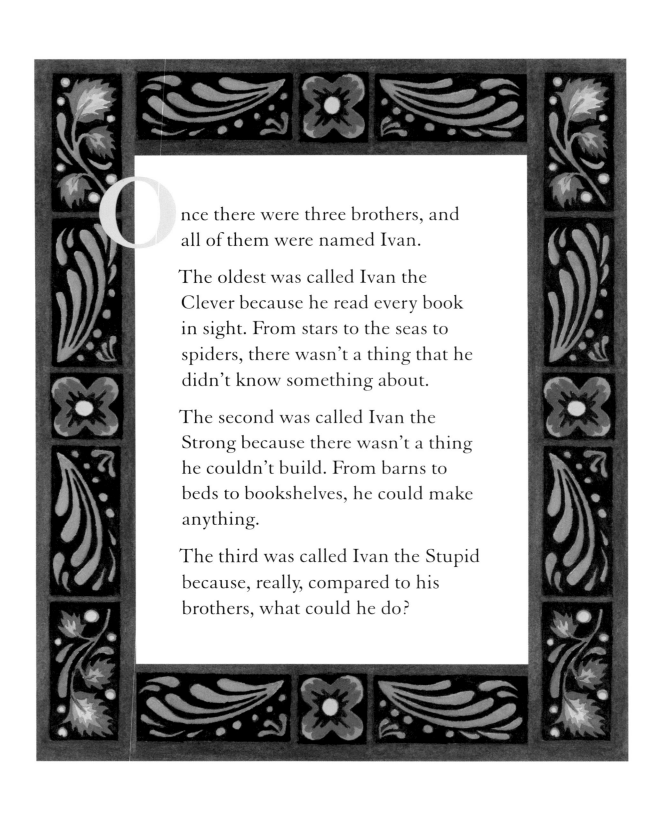

Once there were three brothers, and all of them were named Ivan.

The oldest was called Ivan the Clever because he read every book in sight. From stars to the seas to spiders, there wasn't a thing that he didn't know something about.

The second was called Ivan the Strong because there wasn't a thing he couldn't build. From barns to beds to bookshelves, he could make anything.

The third was called Ivan the Stupid because, really, compared to his brothers, what could he do?

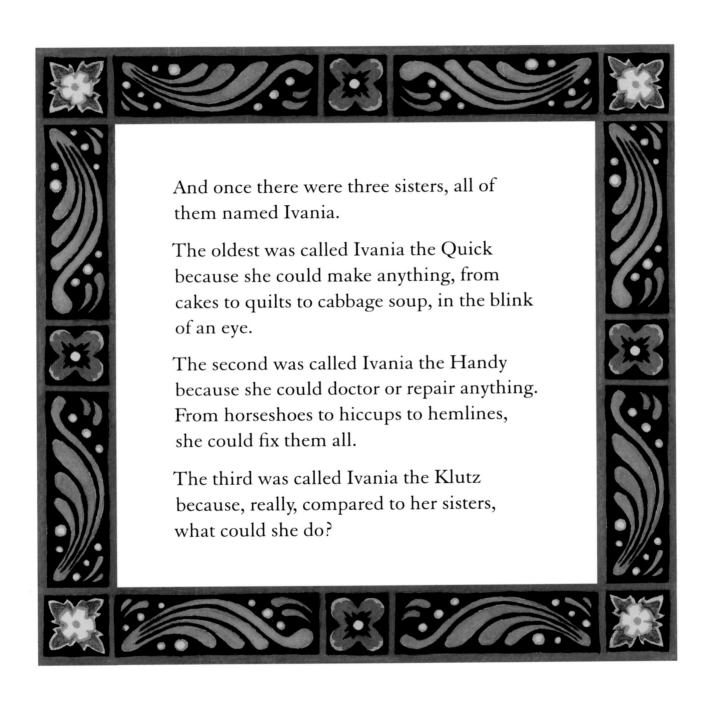

And once there were three sisters, all of them named Ivania.

The oldest was called Ivania the Quick because she could make anything, from cakes to quilts to cabbage soup, in the blink of an eye.

The second was called Ivania the Handy because she could doctor or repair anything. From horseshoes to hiccups to hemlines, she could fix them all.

The third was called Ivania the Klutz because, really, compared to her sisters, what could she do?

The brothers had an old Baba,
and so did the sisters.
The two Babas had been friends
for a long time.

"We should play matchmakers," they said.

So the Babas introduced Ivan the Clever to Ivania the Quick, and it was love at first sight, with a wedding soon after.

The Babas beamed. "How nice!"

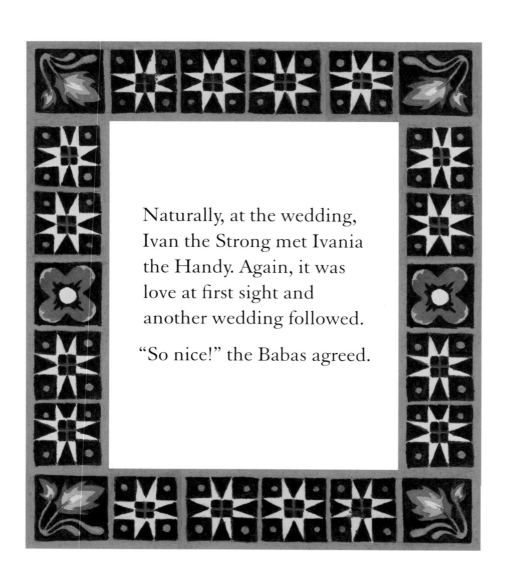

Naturally, at the wedding, Ivan the Strong met Ivania the Handy. Again, it was love at first sight and another wedding followed.

"So nice!" the Babas agreed.

Despite dancing together at two weddings,
Ivan the Stupid and Ivania the Klutz ignored each other.

"Hmmm," said the Babas.
"We must give them a task to do together."

"Here," said the Babas to Ivan the Stupid and Ivania the Klutz. "See this field scattered with poppy seeds? Go and gather up all the seeds."

"Do what?" said Ivan.

"That's crazy!" said Ivania, and they went their separate ways.

The family all sighed.
"It was such a romantic idea!
Like an old fairy tale."

"That's what we thought,"
the disappointed Babas said.
"The rest of you need to
help with this."

"Let's have them watch our twin babies,"
said Ivania the Quick.

"Absolutely," said Ivan the Clever. "Then
they will want to have a family of their own."

So Ivan the Stupid and Ivania the Klutz
did the babysitting.

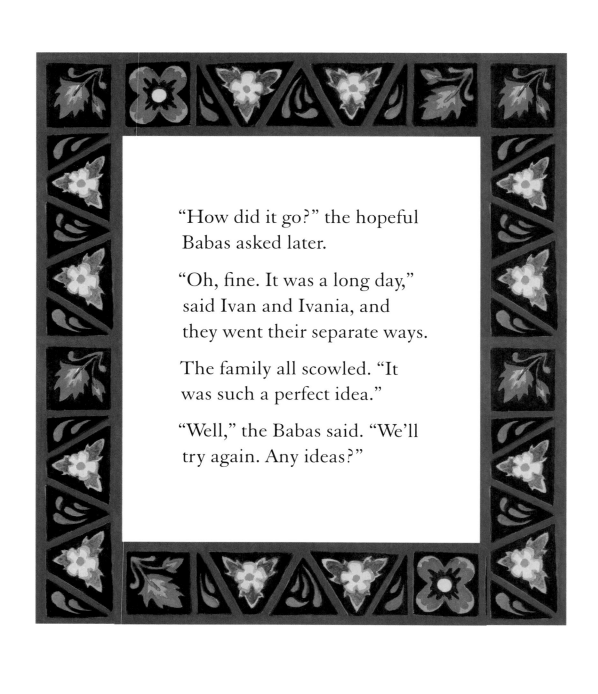

"How did it go?" the hopeful
Babas asked later.

"Oh, fine. It was a long day,"
said Ivan and Ivania, and
they went their separate ways.

The family all scowled. "It
was such a perfect idea."

"Well," the Babas said. "We'll
try again. Any ideas?"

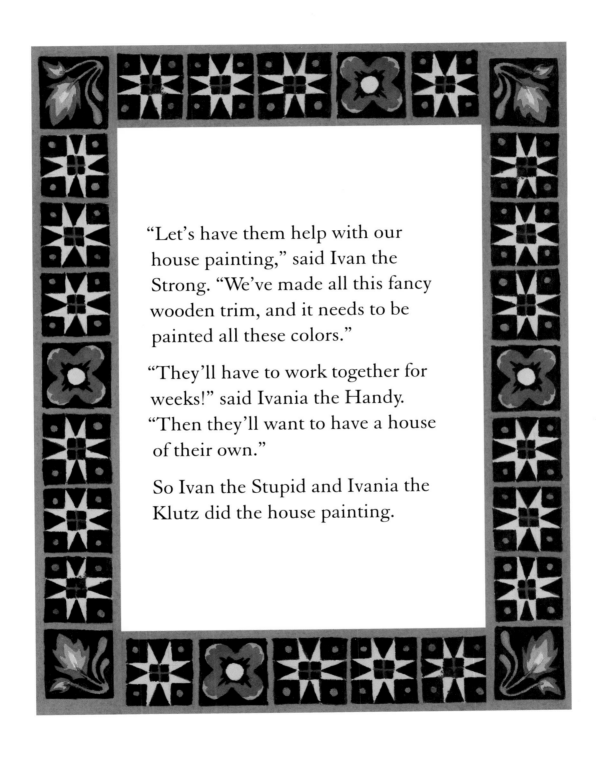

"Let's have them help with our house painting," said Ivan the Strong. "We've made all this fancy wooden trim, and it needs to be painted all these colors."

"They'll have to work together for weeks!" said Ivania the Handy. "Then they'll want to have a house of their own."

So Ivan the Stupid and Ivania the Klutz did the house painting.

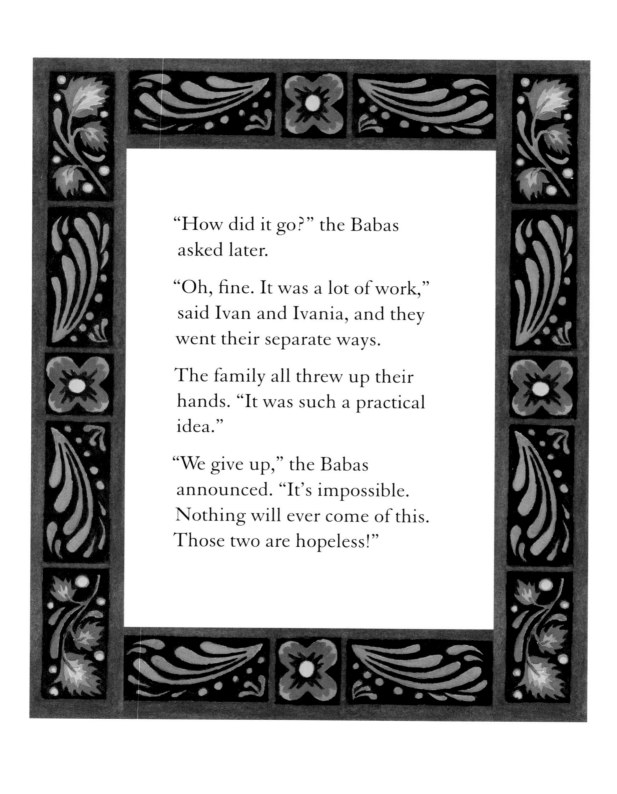

"How did it go?" the Babas
asked later.

"Oh, fine. It was a lot of work,"
said Ivan and Ivania, and they
went their separate ways.

The family all threw up their
hands. "It was such a practical
idea."

"We give up," the Babas
announced. "It's impossible.
Nothing will ever come of this.
Those two are hopeless!"

By this time the poppy seeds in the field had rested and sprouted and grown and budded and were blooming gloriously.

"Weeds!" grumbled most of the family.

But Ivan the Stupid and Ivania the Klutz happened to meet in the field of poppy flowers.

"It's just as well that we didn't pick up all the seeds," they agreed. "This is beautiful!"

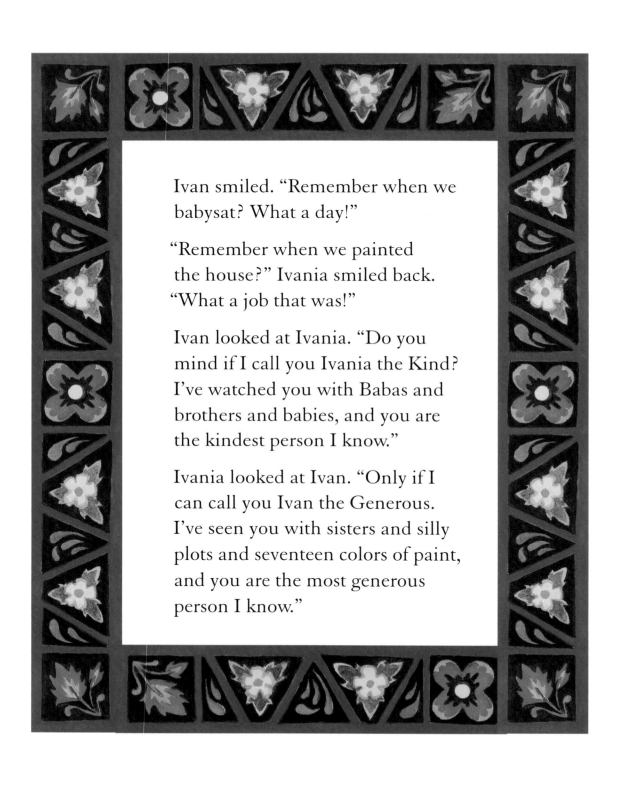

Ivan smiled. "Remember when we babysat? What a day!"

"Remember when we painted the house?" Ivania smiled back. "What a job that was!"

Ivan looked at Ivania. "Do you mind if I call you Ivania the Kind? I've watched you with Babas and brothers and babies, and you are the kindest person I know."

Ivania looked at Ivan. "Only if I can call you Ivan the Generous. I've seen you with sisters and silly plots and seventeen colors of paint, and you are the most generous person I know."

Ivan the Generous and Ivania the Kind held hands
and walked on together in the field of poppies.

The family watched them from far away.

"See! Just like we always said," the Babas pointed out.
"Everything in its own good time."

A Note from the Author

This is an original story, but it incorporates many of the things usually found in Russian fairy tales—heroes named Ivan, third-born children, Babas, and innumerable difficult tasks. No talking animals or dolls, though. I hope you will search out some of the old Russian tales, such as "The Firebird," "Maria Morevna," "The Snow Maiden," and "Vassilissa the Fair."

Besides Russian fairy tales, I like gardening, making Ukrainian eggs, and doing Sudoku puzzles. Other books I have written are *Ida May's Borrowed Trouble, Beasties, Gloppy, Digital Girl and the Greenish Ghosts,* and *The Secret of Santa's Naughty-Nice List.*

Many thanks to Rachael for the marvelous illustrations, and to the Book Bridge Press team—Aimee, Lois, Helga, and Darrin. Thanks also to family and friends who gave encouragement and feedback along the way—Christina, Emmeline, Paulina, Becky, Donna and her family, and Yuri. Last but not least, thanks to Tom, who is both kind and generous.

Rachael Balsaitis

Rachael is an illustrator from Minneapolis, Minnesota, with family roots in the country of Lithuania. She lives with her little critters, and loves a good book and a cup of coffee on a rainy day.